The Race for the
Chinese Zodiac

For Emma and Jack, our little Rooster and Rat – GW
For all Goats, friendly, creative and a little bit crazy – RA

First published in the UK 2012 by Walker Books Ltd
87 Vauxhall Walk, London SE11 5HJ

First published 2010

10 9 8 7 6 5 4 3 2 1

Printed in China

British Library Cataloguing in Publication Data:
a catalogue record for this book is available from the British Library

ISBN 978-1-4063-4698-5

www.walker.co.uk

The Race for the Chinese Zodiac

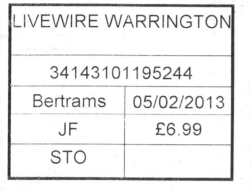

by Gabrielle Wang

illustrated by

Sally Rippin and Regine Abos

WALKER BOOKS
AND SUBSIDIARIES
LONDON · BOSTON · SYDNEY · AUCKLAND

Long ago in ancient China, Jade Emperor,
who was ruler of Heaven and Earth,
proclaimed a mighty race.
"The first twelve animals to cross the river
will each have a year named after them,"
he announced.

The animals lined up along the shore
eager to begin.
The waters slapped and swirled.
The mountains trembled.
Jade Emperor's gong rang out.

Courageous Tiger leaped into the river,
striking out with his powerful paws.

Peaceful Rabbit jumped onto a log,
holding on with all her might.

Charming Rat and Friendly Cat
did everything together.
"Take us across on your
back, Ox, and we will
show you the way."
Kind Ox agreed
and they climbed
on board.

鼠猫牛

Faithful Dog played in the shallows,
jumping and splashing and chasing his shadow.

Lucky Rooster found a raft.
"Who will give me a hand?" he asked.
"I will," said Clever Monkey and he cleared
the reeds. Then Gentle Goat pushed the raft
into the water.

Spirited Horse plunged into the river,
hooves churning mud from the riverbed.
But who was hiding in Horse's mane?
It was Wise Snake, getting a free ride!

Happy Pig put her toe in the water.
Then drew it out again. "I'm hungry,
I need something to eat," she said.
So Pig ate and ate and ate until her
tummy was as

big as a balloon.

Then she fell asleep in the mud.

Powerful Dragon flew out
across the river, scales shimmering
like pearls in the sun.
The clouds parted. Thunder rumbled,
shaking the mountain tops.

"We're winning!" cried Rat.
When Cat stood up to look,
Rat pushed her into the water.

bank,

.

eclared.

"Why so slow, Tiger?" Rabbit called out.
"I was carried downstream on
a strong current," Tiger replied.
"But I'm back on course now!"

Just then, a breath of wind blew Rabbit
all the way to shore.
She leaped off her log and hopped
across the finish line, right behind Tiger.

Next came Dragon swooping down
from the sky. "What held you up?"
Jade Emperor asked.
"I saw people and animals suffering
a terrible drought so I stopped
to make rain," Dragon replied.

"Then I saw a poor little rabbit clinging
to a log and blew her to the shore."
"You have a kind heart. The fifth year
of the Zodiac will be named after you,"
Jade Emperor declared.

Horse galloped towards the finish line.
I'm next, she thought. But at the last
second, Snake sprang to the ground
beating Horse by a flicker of his tongue.

Goat, Monkey and Rooster jumped off
their raft. "You three work well together,"
Jade Emperor said. "In eighth, ninth and
tenth places will be the years of the Goat,
Monkey and Rooster."

Dog dashed towards the emperor, wagging his stumpy tail. "I was playing in the shallows and almost forgot the race," he barked.

Jade Emperor smiled. "The eleventh year will be named after you, little dog."

After waking from a long nap, Pig floated across on her tummy.
"You have done well too," Jade Emperor said. "And so, the final spot on the Zodiac belongs to you."

29

Poor Cat dragged herself up on the bank.
But she was too late. There are only twelve
places on the Chinese Zodiac.

And that is why, to this very day,
cats have hated rats.

The Twelve Animals
of the Chinese Zodiac

Rat: 1924, 1936, 1948, 1960, 1972, 1984, 1996, 2008, 2020, 2032
Rats are intelligent and have big imaginations. They are strong-willed, idealistic, ambitious, tolerant and charming. They like people therefore they have lots of friends. They also like collecting things.

Ox: 1925, 1937, 1949, 1961, 1973, 1985, 1997, 2009, 2021, 2033
Oxen like to be leaders. They are hardworking, dependable, sociable, patient and honest. Oxen can be artistic and love being outside in nature.

Tiger: 1926, 1938, 1950, 1962, 1974, 1986, 1998, 2010, 2022, 2034
Tigers are brave and like adventure. They are determined, courageous, generous, sympathetic and also like joking around. Tigers can be lucky with money.

Rabbit: 1927, 1939, 1951, 1963, 1975, 1987, 1999, 2011, 2023, 2035
Out of all the animal signs, Rabbits make the best friends. This is because they are peace-loving creatures. They are happy, gifted, ambitious, virtuous, thoughtful and are attracted to beautiful things.

Dragon: 1928, 1940, 1952, 1964, 1976, 1988, 2000, 2012, 2024, 2036
Dragons are natural leaders with strong personalities. They have lots of energy and are full of bright ideas. They are passionate, vibrant and brave and like to be in the middle of the action.

Snake: 1929, 1941, 1953, 1965, 1977, 1989, 2001, 2013, 2025, 2037
Snakes are wise and innovative. They are also patient, philosophical, diplomatic and deep thinkers. They have good imaginations and can be artistic. Snakes like to laugh and make other people laugh with them.

Horse: 1930, 1942, 1954, 1966, 1978, 1990, 2002, 2014, 2026, 2038

Horses are funny, popular, fearless and hardworking. They like playing sport because they have lots of energy. They are also confident, spirited, honest, sensitive and brave. Horses like helping others.

Goat: 1931, 1943, 1955, 1967, 1979, 1991, 2003, 2015, 2027, 2039

Goats are peaceful, friendly, gentle and easygoing. They have good imaginations and love anything artistic. They are also sensitive, modest, creative and generous.

Monkey: 1932, 1944, 1956, 1968, 1980, 1992, 2004, 2016, 2028, 2040

Monkeys are very clever and gifted in everything they do. They are mischievous, funny, reliable, inventive and honest and they like being with people.

Rooster: 1933, 1945, 1957, 1969, 1981, 1993, 2005, 2017, 2029, 2041

Roosters are easygoing and never shy. They like reading and travelling so they are very knowledgeable. They also have good memories and are brave, resilient, independent and lucky.

Dog: 1934, 1946, 1958, 1970, 1982, 1994, 2006, 2018, 2030, 2042

Dogs are faithful, loyal and unselfish. They are steady workers, dependable, patient, modest, intelligent and caring. They make great friends because they will always stand by you.

Pig: 1935, 1947, 1959, 1971, 1983, 1995, 2007, 2019, 2031, 2043

Pigs always try to do what is right. They are popular and tolerant and great fun to be with. They are peace-loving, lucky, honest and patient and also love their food.

(Because this is a lunar calendar, birthdays between January and February may change from year to year. In this case, consult a Chinese calendar.)